# The Tickle Tree

Written by Chae Strathie and illustrated by Poly Bernatene

PaRragon

Bath · New York · Singapore · Hong Kong · Cologne · Delhi
Melbourne · Amsterdam · Johannesburg · Shenzhen

Have you ever been there
where the Tickle Tree grows...

...and laughed as it jiggles its twigs on your toes?

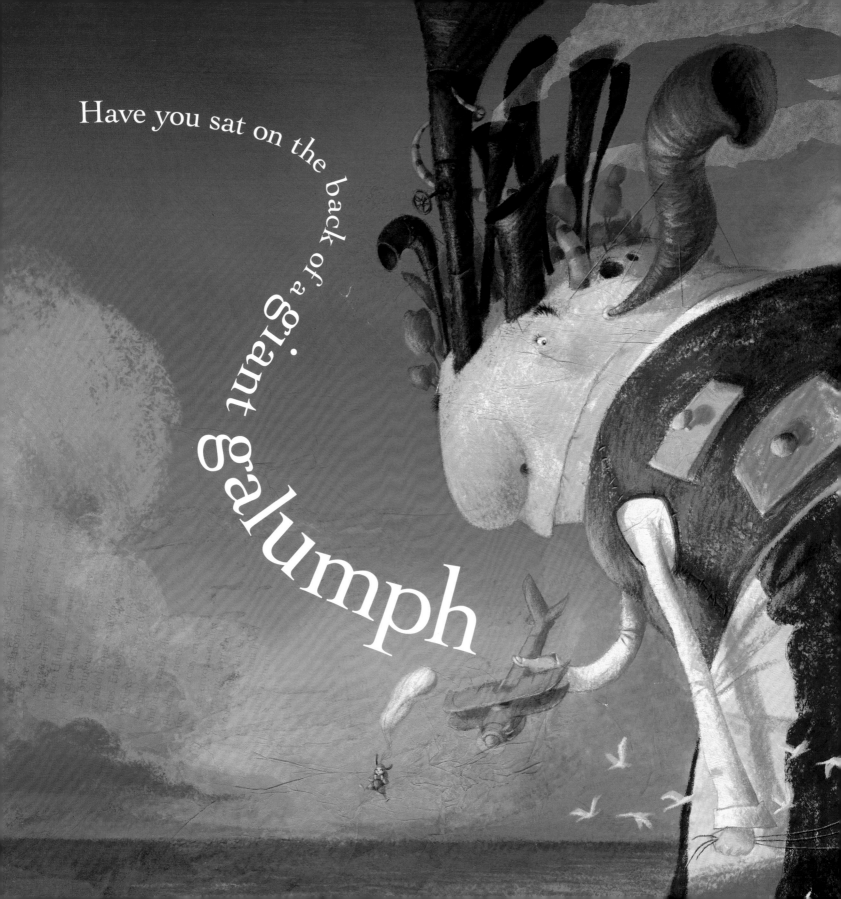

Have you sat on the back of a giant galumph

and let out a " whoop " as you slid down its hump?

Have you scratched an old crabbysnap under its chin

or slept through the sound of a boomjangle's din?

Have you walked with a wibblebird made out of jelly

or perched on the paunch of a blubbalub's belly?

If the answer is **no,**
then you shouldn't despair,
as I'm sure that there's some way
for you to get there.

Have you leaped like a springbungle up to the stars and said "howdy-do!" to the Grimbles on Mars?

Have you wondered why horse-riding

Or played hide-and-seek with a luminous frink?

poo-munkles stink?

To get there is simple,
but you'll have to wait
and hope that I tell you
**before it's too late!**

Have you given a moonjack a ride on your foot, or cuddled a clumph and been hugged by a snoot?

If the answer is no, then that's really tough luck. Without clear directions, it looks like you're stuck.

Have you danced with a marvelous musical meep
or dunked with a dennyfish
down in the deep?

Have you had a **pink** puffalunk's last piece of pie or climbed a free **fangdangle** up to the sky?

Don't tell me
you haven't,
I'm really surprised.

All right, then,
I'll show you, but first
close your eyes.

It's clear that you're eager to get to this place, where snugglebugs buzz and ripunzelruns race.

I'll show you the way, but it's not where it seems.

Through the Tickle Tree's leaves and...

...into your dreams!

With love to my mum Gill
and my dad Calum,
and not forgetting Eilidh,
who's at the heart of every book.

C.S.


For my children,
who teach me how to fly...

P.B.

This edition published by Parragon Books Ltd in 2013 and distributed by Parragon Inc.

440 Park Avenue Sound, 13th Floor
New York, NY 10016
www.parragon.com

Published by arrangement with Meadowside Children's Books

Text : © Chae Strathie 2008
Illustrations: © Poly Bernatene 2008

ISBN 978-1-4723-3592-0

Printed in China